T0208797

Life in

ЯEVERSE

Life in ЯEVERSE

A ROAD TO DEAFIESBURG, DEAFYLAND

ARTHUR GRANT DIGNAN

ARCHWAY PUBLISHING

Archway Publishing books may be ordered through booksellers or by contacting:

Archway Publishing
1663 Liberty Drive
Bloomington, IN 47403
www.archwaypublishing.com
844-669-3957

ISBN: 978-1-6657-3525-4 (sc)
ISBN: 978-1-6657-3526-1 (hc)
ISBN: 978-1-6657-3527-8 (e)

Library of Congress Control Number: 2022923166

Print information available on the last page.

Archway Publishing rev. date: 12/23/2022

Contents

Thank Yous

I wouldn't have been able to finish this book if it weren't for the people I'm mentioning here. I started writing over 20 years ago, stopped, and never got back to it until recently with the help of my darling daughter, Jennifer Dignan Morales. She pushed and pushed for me to finish it. She sat by me as she and I worked on the book for hours. Thank you, my dear Jenny! I love you dearly!

I wanted an outside person to proofread it, and I chose one of my closest friends, Larry R. Hoard. He has been one of my biggest supporters and is one of my most cherished friends. I couldn't have finished this book without his help and his wisdom. Thank you, my buddy! I love you!

Mistie, thank you for your help with a few things in the book. We appreciate you more than you know! You're a dear friend of ours!

I also couldn't have done it without the support of my sons; Randy & Nick, their wives; Janelle and Ashley, my daughter's husband; Jorge, my grandchildren; Briella, Rayana, Grant,

Clara, Cade, Madelyn, Colt, McKinley, Amelia, Benton, Conan, Darrion, and one more on the way. Briella, my oldest granddaughter, helped with the finishing touches of my book. Thank you, my dear, Briella! My daughter in law, Ashley, also helped a lot with her inputs. My other daughter in law, Janelle, asked me a few times throughout the years when I would finish the book. I appreciated the gentle push. I love you all very much!

Lastly, the one person behind me all the way, the love of my life, my number one supporter; my wife, Joyce. I couldn't have done everything in my life without her support. She's my backbone! Thank you, my dear darling, Joyce! I love you very much!

Thank you, to the people at Archway Publishing, for helping me through the publication process.

Introduction

The State and the City

Deafiesburg, Deafyland, is often overlooked by ordinary citizens because it is a unique state located in a region of the United States of America that is not yet included on the map. However, the state is also unique because it has all the landscapes that people love, such as mountains, open fields, lakes, rivers, and the ocean. When first stepping into the state, every tourist, oblivious to its name and unaware of its differences in language and culture, would say, "Wow, what a beautiful state! I wonder if they have a job available for me here."

Deafyland has snow-covered mountains, many different kinds of trees, and beautiful resorts that are available for all winter sport events. The state is 3,712 square miles, with 531 square miles of inland water and twenty-one miles of coastal water.

The state's soil is rich and produces the best-tasting vegetables and fruits, especially pears. The state's agriculture also includes eggs, cattle, hogs, sheep, chicken, and turkey. It has some of the finest dairy cows in the country. Along the coastline, there are a prosperous fishing industry and deaf farmers. Fishermen are the most prominent investors. Annually, businesspeople from other states and countries come to Deafyland to study its farming methods. Deafyland's series of instructional books, Raising Food in a Simple Way, are on the best seller's list. Unknown to the readers, the books are written by deaf authors who profess English as their second language. Their native language is American Sign Language (ASL).

In 2010, Deafyland's population was estimated to be about nine hundred thousand deaf individuals and about 135,000 nondeaf residents. The deaf residents make up more than 85 percent of Deafyland's population. Powerful deaf politicians dominate the autonomous state and local governments. In 1990, the national government granted the deaf people the authority to run the state fully autonomous, following the request by a noble deaf leader named Benjamin Hirsch. He, along with some of his deaf mentors, founded Deafyland in 1970. They realized that the deaf language and cultural views were not the same as hearing languages and cultures. The state was based on the time when it was proposed. That small group of deaf ancestors recognized the needs of their culture and language. However, the agreement was that the state would abide by the national constitution and bylaws like other states, except for the differences in language and culture. The deaf ancestors vowed to maintain tax expenditures with the national government. As a result, Deafyland promptly united with the national country that same year, 1990.

Deafiesburg is the capital of Deafyland and is the largest city in the state. It's in the center of the state. It is the ideal place because it is accessible to travelers who commute from other parts of the state. The city is an industrial and banking center. It has a headquarters, where deaf people are considered the majority instead of a minority.

Hirschville is the second largest city. It bears the name in honor of Benjamin Hirsch's invaluable contributions and most noble character. It has many beautiful harbors, which serve the fishing industry; beach resorts; and is sponsored by the most prominent Deaf Yacht Association. Many fabulous seafood restaurants, souvenir shops, and museums can be seen along the exclusive seaport wharf.

The state's communication system serves and is based on its majority's needs. It has evolved alongside the growing civilization. The primary and legal language, ASL, is a visual language, not a written or spoken language. However, deaf voters recognize the importance of maintaining good relationships with states where English is the primary and legal language. They fully support providing English as a second language in all of Deafyland's public schools. The nondeaf students who reside in Deafyland are required to learn ASL as their second language. Deafyland strictly enforces ASL as the state's primary language. Often, some nondeaf students protest that ASL is the most difficult language to learn.

Deafyland was admitted to the United States around the same time that the deaf leaders were able to establish the state. The one condition that Benjamin Hirsch and the other deaf mentors had was that it be governed autonomously and indefinitely by deaf people. The request was approved by the national government during the same month, merely four days prior to the declaration of the union. The opening constitutional statement read, "Of the deaf people, by the deaf people, for the deaf people," rather than "of the deaf people, by the hearing people, for the deaf people," which is observed by the other states. The state motto is this: "If you cherish your culture, cherish your language also." The state song, "Deaf-Deaf, People-People, People," with the famous one-two, one-two-three rhythm was developed by Mr. B. B. Miracle.

In 1990, Deafyland adopted a constitution, which combined elements from the national constitution with Deafyland's revisions. Proposals to amend the constitution are made at the state's annual constitutional convention. Amendments require approval by two-thirds of the members from each house of legislature. If approved, amendments will be voted on in the next general election. To be received into law, the amendments must receive approval from a majority of the voters.

Deafyland welcomes tourists. For further information, you can write to the Deafyland Tourist Center at 2001 Capitol Way, Deafiesburg, DD, 90030, or video call (800) 440-7000. The number for nondeaf people is (800) 440-7314. An interpreter will translate ASL to English and vice versa, allowing hearing viewers to communicate with the deaf people in the official ASL language.

1

ON THE ROAD TO DEAFIESBURG

On a warm Monday afternoon in July, on Highway 17, the hearing-able Braden family marveled at the beautiful landscape and sweet aroma while crossing the state line into Deafyland. They were the only car on the highway. It was their last week of a month-long vacation. Many beautiful blue ponds were seen on both sides of the highway, and the landscape reflected off their surfaces like mirrors. The green fields over the rolling hills were well cultivated. The farm buildings revealed the builders' skillful craftsmanship. The family was tired, but the scenery restored them with enough energy to continue vacationing. The gorgeous welcome sign, which was overlooked by the family, read, "Welcome to a unique state, Deafyland! We cordially invite you to enjoy your visit in our state." Upcoming events and information about resorts were clearly presented on billboards in ASL.

The Bradens were excited to be on their way home. Paul

Braden, a husky and handsome former all-state and national athlete, was at the wheel. He was well dressed in his usual, expensive English-style summer outfit and Italian-made sandals. For a man in his midfifties, his physique could fool anyone. Most would think he was as young as thirty years old. He was a vice president at a bank and had been with that same bank for twenty-two years. The bank's board of trustees had recently appointed him as first vice president for the same firm, beginning in the upcoming new year.

The people in town loved and trusted him. Paul knew how to help his patrons and had successfully assisted every business associated with the bank. His office walls were covered with numerous plaques that he had been awarded and pictures of himself posing with important and recognizable people from his home state. On his desk, an enormous framed picture of his beloved family stood next to a gold double pen stand labelled, "Most outstanding banker of the year." New customers were always referred to him, even though other banks were available in the largely populated town of 250,000.

His lovely wife, Mary, glanced at him with a continuous smile. A mother to their three children, she was forty-eight, but like Paul, many people mistook her for thirty years old. She sat next to Paul, her fingers fondling the back of his hair. She wore a white summer dress with bright blue spots, which matched her beautiful blue eyes. She had a pair of soles with strings that went from the bottom to above her ankles. Her daughters wore the same style of shoes.

Mary was a full-time housewife and a very active president

for the town's women's society. She was also involved in many other organizations, for which she received many awards. As a teenager, Mary had volunteered as an aide for an underachiever juvenile program and had won the junior beauty pageant hosted by the town's chamber of commerce. Two years ago, the state had recognized and honored Mary's countless contributions to the community with an award. Paul and Mary had met and fallen in love in college, where Paul had graduated with a business administration degree.

The children were sitting on the backbenches of the light blue van. The oldest daughter, Amy, was sixteen years old and in the tenth grade. She looked like her mother, but she had her father's brown eyes and hair. Amy had been thinking about majoring in psychology when she went to college. She was one of the top ten students her class. She sat on the rear bench seat with her ten-year-old sister, Toni. Toni looked up to Amy and wanted to be exactly like her big sister. Amy was the captain of the girls' varsity volleyball team and cocaptain of the cheerleading squad. The school encouraged her parents to have Amy apply for the governor's special scholarship program before her senior year. That program would grant an annual amount of $5,000 toward her college tuition if she completed three academic activities, each six weeks.

Joe, their twelve-year-old son, was one of the most active and athletic boys in his seventh-grade class. He sat alone on the middle bench seat behind his father, whispering to him in a gruff voice. Football and basketball were his favorite sports. He dreamed of someday winning a scholarship to a division-one university for either sport. He wanted to follow in his father's footsteps. Paul had been a basketball star in both high school and college. He had taught Joe all about sports. They went to many games together. Joe's peers always wanted him on their team, because he contributed to most of the wins.

Toni was a fifth grader. She rested her head on Amy's shoulder. Toni was fond of music. Her friends called her the school counselor's aide. She always helped her classmates solve their problems. Sometimes Toni solved their problems before they saw the school counselor. She wore the same dress as her mother, but her hair was like Amy's.

In the back of the vehicle, through the rear window, one could see chips, cookies, and fruit on top of some luggage. A luggage carrier was visible on top of the vehicle. On the bumper, there was an old, worn-out decal reading, "My daughter is a ninth-grade honor student at Kirby High School." On the rear door, there were many new decals from different sites that the family had toured recently.

The family talked about their friends back home, who they missed. They were excited to be heading home soon so they could tell everyone about their one-month-long vacation. The family was reminded to think hard about where to go next year, because Paul would have a five-week-long vacation after assuming the new position.

While driving, Paul discussed how the bank was doing during his absence. Mary wrote up an agenda for the next women's society meeting in two weeks. Amy was excited that she would soon see her two best friends and the cute boy she had begun dating. Joe was still sad about missing three baseball games for the vacation. Paul brightened Joe's mood by telling him the weather app on his phone reported that it had been raining in their hometown on the game days and that the games were probably rescheduled. Toni was still resting, but she eavesdropped on the conversation at times.

"Daddy," exclaimed Joe, "any idea where we will go on our next vacation, since we it's going to be five weeks long?"

Paul was about to speak when Amy interrupted. "How about Washington, DC, and all the places surrounding it? I was told that it would take months to really see everything."

"Amy, let Daddy talk now," said Mary. "He was going to say something, but you interrupted. Darling Paul, what was it you wanted to say?"

After Amy's apology, Paul said, "It's funny; I was going to suggest what she suggested. I feel it's time for you children to learn all about how our government runs the country and to visit all the historical sights and the museums there. They have one museum that focuses on old cars. I would like to visit it. I hope to see some of the cars that I rode in when I was a kid."

Amy shot back excitedly, "Great minds think alike. Mommy, I read some books that said they preserve all the presidents' and their wives' belongings in one of those museums. Maybe we could get some ideas for the cloth patterns from them."

"But Daddy and I always think alike more than you do, because we are men," Joe protested jokingly.

Paul chuckled. "Oh, my Joe, don't be a male chauvinist."

Mary scolded with a smile, "We'll talk about our next vacation soon and plan it when the time comes. And, Amy, yes, you are right about the clothes. I saw them on my high school senior trip a long time ago, but I heard they've added so much more now."

"We could split the five-week vacation into two and half weeks in Washington, DC, and the remaining at a different time and location if we wanted to," reminded Paul.

"That's neat, Dad!" exclaimed Joe.

Suddenly, Paul realized that he had not paid much attention to the highway signs for a few hours and had lost track of where they were. He feared that they were lost. "Oh no, where are we? I can't recall the name of this state, except the sign said something like, 'Welcome to the unique state, D— We cordially invite you to—' Did any of you see the name of the state by chance? Are we still on Highway 17?"

Everyone began to murmur. Mary looked at Paul and asked, "Why did you turn off the GPS on your phone?"

Paul sighed. "I was checking the weather app."

Toni was wide awake and, as expected at her age, curious. Paul was frustrated that he'd taken the wrong route, but he willingly accepted responsibility for not paying attention to the road signs. The scenery was still very beautiful with the green trees, fields, rolling hills, and the white fence that ran alongside the road. The farms were very neat and well cared for. While Paul wondered about the wrong route, Mary picked up her iPhone and checked to see whether they were still on Highway 17. The family began to search for signs along the road in this strange area.

Amy came up with a notion and uttered vaguely, "I

think I glimpsed the state name. The first few letters were something like *D-E-A* …"

Joe predicted, "Well, we will enjoy one more attractive site on our way home."

Paul said, "I believe the last route I saw was Highway 17 … Or was it 27?"

Toni screamed, "There's a sign coming up! What does it say?"

"No need to scream that loud," Joe complained. "Farmers out there could hear your hollering."

"The name of the city is Deafiesburg," explained Amy. "The sign reads, 'Deafiesburg city limit, fifty miles.'"

Paul turned to Mary and asked, "Honey, would you please look for more information on the *Traveling Yours* app on your phone and see which state it's in? I vaguely remember hearing about it. That name is odd."

"How exactly do you say that word, *Deafiesburg*?" wondered Mary.

Amy giggled. "Looks like it's a town full of weird people who are deaf and dumb." She turned to Joe, chuckling. "I don't think there will be anything exciting to look at in that town."

"Amy," said Mary, "don't jump to conclusions; let me look it up in the app." As she turned to her phone, Joe gazed out at the gorgeous scenery and started counting the trees on one side of the rolling hills. Toni was getting ready to snooze off again. The rest of the family waited.

Paul said, "Maybe, Amy is right. The first part of that word is deaf."

"Yeah, right" Joe murmured and rolled his eyes.

"Yes, yes," interrupted Mary. "I found the information. The town is in a state called Deafyland, and we are still on Highway 17."

"I believe I have heard of this state before," said Paul. "When I was in elementary school, we studied all the states, but it didn't exist then."

Amy recalled, "I had a teacher who taught us about the states. One of my classmates asked if we'd study this one. She said it was a small state and there was nothing to learn about it."

"It has a population of nine hundred thousand deaf residents and a few nondeaf people," quoted Mary. "Look, here is a special article on the state's brief history. Want me to read it aloud to you all, darlings?"

"Oh no!" Alarmed, Toni suddenly sat up. "I heard from some friends that the deaf people are crazy. When they talk, they make funny faces and move their hands. Their faces are like the aliens'. Some of them scream with strange, loud voices. Daddy, please turn back. I don't want to see them."

"There was a poor, little deaf girl named Teresa in my sixth-grade class," recalled Amy. "Someone told me she could not communicate with her parents. The school suggested that she go to the school for the deaf, but her parents refused, because they considered the deaf school very low and without language. I remember seeing her so lonely, sat alone in the corner at lunch every day. She was placed in a room with other handicapped children, because the woman there was a special education teacher. Whenever I walked by the room,

I would always see her sitting there, doing nothing. She was very isolated. From that observation, I don't believe there is hope for any deaf child like that. That teacher apparently did not know how to communicate with Teresa, so she decided to abandon her to the corner."

"Oh, what a pity," said Mary sympathetically. "I've heard many times that deaf children are worse than other handicapped children. Once I met a special education teacher too. That teacher said she could help children who had the same communication as us, but deaf children did not have any communication at all. She said there was no hope for them, because their mode of communication was very limited. She couldn't do anything with them but let them play in the room on their own. I feel so sorry for them, no future at all."

"Mom," Toni asked, "what does limited communication mean?"

"It means incomplete or not perfect. Faulty," interrupted Amy. Mary nodded approvingly.

Joe added, "Yes, someone told me that they make funny faces while waving their hands, and their communication obviously makes no sense at all. Their voices are unintelligible."

Toni repeated hysterically, "Oh, Daddy, please turn around now. I'm so afraid."

Paul grinned and turned to Toni. "Let's listen to the brief history of the town first. There's no need to be alarmed. Remember they are disabled. I'm kind of curious now."

Amy said, "Mom, please read the article. Maybe we will be able to just go by the town. I'm curious about the history, and I think we will enjoy watching those clowns as we pass through."

"Ha! OK, Amy, let's be quiet," said Mary. "Darling Toni, don't worry. We are with you. I will read now." Mary looked at her phone and read, "Deafyland was founded in 1990, by a group of deaf farmers. Before springtime that year, they came from different places in Deafyland, meeting in a small town, where the most notable deaf leader Benjamin Hirsch lived. The meeting was held at a small tavern. The communication observed there did not involve speech but sign language. They griped that the smaller population of nondeaf people who lived in the town would not support or accept deaf people's right to have their own culture and language. The nondeaf people denied and vetoed many proposals to establish a deaf community. They were influenced by the foreigners' philosophy of oral practice for the deaf and believed that with enforced training, the deaf people could learn how to speak and lip-read their spoken language. They believed that eventually deaf people would be capable of functioning well in the nondeaf community.

"One member argued that it would be like the nondeaf training the blind to see. Benjamin added that the nondeaf ignored the fact that once an old philosopher said, 'So if there was a language, there was a culture.' His son, Benjamin Jr., felt like he was being treated unfairly by nondeaf people in the same way African Americans or Native Americans were treated unfairly by white people. Another member explained that as a minority group, it would always be difficult to accomplish anything.

"One person asked whether or not deaf people usually had unpleasant attitudes and if that was the reason the nondeaf were uncooperative. A deaf farmer expressed deep concern that his six deaf children would be miseducated, because his request for a more accessible education had been denied by the nondeaf school board. A deaf construction worker shared that most nondeaf educators believed forcing the oral method on deaf pupils was very effective. The deaf people knew that this was not the case for the majority of the deaf.

"Mrs. Hirsh, the wife of Benjamin and mother of Benjamin Jr., remarked that the barriers they were facing had been an ongoing problem for many years. The International Nondeaf Educators of the Deaf Conference was held somewhere in Germany. It had voted to ban the use of sign language and the hiring of deaf teachers in each country. They hadn't invited any deaf professionals to participate. With that new law, they had asked the deaf teachers to leave their positions promptly. Mrs. Taylor, the construction worker's wife, commented that she feared deaf people's miserable lives and that it was doomsday for the deaf members.

"Everyone at the meeting was very angry that nondeaf people were oppressing them. The group decided to draw up a petition requesting the government to grant enough land for a new town that deaf people could autonomously govern. They adjourned the meeting with great determination. But Benjamin Hirsch feared that the petition would not work, since the majority would not want to lose their power. Therefore, he donated his four thousand acres of land to implement a deaf community. As the years went by, more deaf people purchased land.

"The small town where the meeting was first held was named Hirschville in honor of Benjamin Hirsch Sr. It was populated by the first 280 deaf people. Then they were granted governance over the town. Some years later, more land was given by the national government. Today the population has increased to nine hundred thousand, and the census has predicted that it will increase to 1.5 million by 2050.

"In October of 2020, the state will mark the thirty-year anniversary of its founding. The celebration will be called the Heritage of the Magnificent State, Deafyland. Mr. Hirsch's grandson, David Hirsch, is the state's current governor. He is the most intelligent and influential Deaf politician."

"That's interesting," Paul said, "but I feel somewhat offended. They call us *nondeaf* and consider us their oppressors. What'd you say, darling?"

"Yes, that word *miserable* is rude," Mary pointed out. "Why would they think of something like that? I feel offended by that too."

Toni added, "Daddy, I told you they sound dangerous. It is absolutely not safe to drive through that town. Please turn around and drive back to the highway, where the normal people are."

"Mom, did you say there were some nondeaf people living there?" asked Amy.

"Yes, Amy." Mary looked at her iPhone and said, "A few nondeaf people."

Amy said, "Obviously, the nondeaf people—oh, let's say

it this way: hearing. The hearing people will eventually take over when their population expands. Those deaf people are probably like that little girl, Teresa."

"Yes, Amy, you're right," said Paul hesitantly. "I imagine they—the deaf people—could not continue running that town for another 150 years."

"But," Joe reminded them, "remember what they said? Something like how they were treated unfairly by us—oops, I mean those nondeaf people—at that time. I would feel the same if I were in their shoes."

"Joe, don't believe everything you read," reminded Amy.

Mary pointed out, "Maybe the people at that time were like that? Today we would not do that. They need all the help they can get from people like us."

They were startled when Paul spoke urgently. "Oh no! A highway patrol car is behind us with flashing lights. What have I done wrong? OK, you guys, please be still, and let me do the talking if he stops me."

2

THE HIGHWAY PATROLMAN

THE PATROL CAR BEGAN TO SLOW DOWN AS IT PASSED THE blue van. With a stern face, the patrolman gestured for Paul to pull the car over onto the shoulder of the road.

Mary asked, "Paul, do you think maybe you were speeding while we discussed the unusual history of Deafyland?"

As they glanced at the sign that read, "Deafiesburg, ten miles," Joe's nodded in agreement.

Amy said, "Oh, boy, Toni's right. The nightmare has just begun."

Paul shot back nervously, "Hold your tongue, Amy. This is our chance to ask the patrolman about the town. Oh my, I hope there will be nothing but a simple warning for whatever he's stopping me for. Please let me do the talking, dear."

As both vehicles pulled over, Amy admired the patrolman's appearance. When he leaped out of his car, his shiny black boots reflected the sunlight. He quickly put on his Canadian-style hat with one hand, carrying a clipboard in the other. As he walked toward them, the whole family studied the good-looking, well-built patrolman in his well-pressed, dark blue uniform. His badge, black belt, holster, and gun were all very neat and shiny. His stern look remained as he approached the van, ignoring Amy's smile through the van's rear window.

Amy softly said, "Oh, what a very good-looking patrolman."

"Hush, Amy," Mary stuttered nervously. "Be careful. He could hear you. Please remember what Dad said."

Paul rolled down the window as the patrolman stopped at his door. Nervously he asked, "What is wrong?"

Toni held Amy's hand tightly. Through the clear glass of the side window behind Paul, Joe admired the well-polished gun only inches from his face.

Everyone in the car was completely silent as the patrolman sternly began to use sign language. *Your license, please*, he signed.

Paul began to speak awkwardly, asking one question right after another. "What did I do wrong? I don't know how to sign. I am sorry, but I would sign if I knew how. Can you read my lips? Or should I speak louder when I talk?" Paul pointed to his mouth, gesturing to ask whether the patrolman could speak or not.

Mary noticed that the patrolman was not wearing hearing aids. Paul glanced at her as she nervously pointed out, "I don't think he can hear you at all. He isn't wearing hearing aids."

The patrolman shook his head and ignored Paul's

struggle to communicate with him. He lowered his head and investigated the inside of the van, apparently searching for other passengers who might be able to sign. As everyone looked at him nervously, he signed with an obviously questioning expression, *Does anyone know sign language?* He pointed to everyone besides Paul.

Amy felt her heart melt as she looked closely at the patrolman's face. He had a perfect profile and was very handsome.

The patrolman noticed tears on Toni's frightened face. He smiled at her with concern. Paul looked at Toni and noticed she had a look of relief after the patrolman's warm smile. Paul wondered if Toni was hesitant about the assumptions that she had made of deaf people.

The patrolman pulled back and began to write on his clipboard. The family presumed was writing because he had realized that no one could sign.

Joe pointed out, "Looks like he was looking to see if one of us could communicate with him but found that none of us know sign language.

Everyone nodded, agreeing with the comment. Mary reminded them to leave the talking to Dad.

"Oh!" exclaimed Paul. "I might have gotten away with it if I could only sign to him."

Toni's tears were drying up, but she still loudly insisted, "Daddy, I told you to turn back. If we had, this never would have happened. Oh, I am afraid." She still felt hesitant.

"Calm down, Toni," whispered Mary, "Please don't

exaggerate. He seems all right. And who knows? He might be playing deaf."

Paul turned back with a jerk as the patrolman handed slid his clipboard through the window. In very beautiful handwriting, the message on the clipboard read, "Please hand me your driver's license and vehicle registration, and then wait for a few minutes. Thank you."

After Paul returned the clipboard with his license and other documents, the patrolman walked back to his still-flashing vehicle. Curious, everyone except Toni moved toward Paul. Simultaneously they asked, "What did he say?"

Shocked, Paul responded, "He wrote beautifully, telling me to give him my license and registration and to please wait."

Mary argued, "Looks like he does not trust us. He looked around at us first and then asked for the license. That was odd. Honestly, I don't think deaf people should have this kind of occupation."

Paul assured her, "Maybe it's acceptable here. Let's look back and see what he's doing."

Everyone except Paul turned to peek at the patrolman from the rear window. So that the patrolman wouldn't notice, Mary insisted that Paul watch through the rearview mirror. Amy nodded in agreement. From the look on her face, Paul could tell that she was glad to look at the patrolman again.

The patrolman glanced quickly at the Braden family. He smirked at their funny and curious faces. They were looking at him just like the other people he had stopped before.

As the family observed the patrolman, they were

dumbfounded. They couldn't figure out what he was doing. The way his fingers were moving, it seemed like he was typing. There was something just slightly visible above the dashboard. He even paused before moving his fingers again.

Toni was nervously puzzled. "What is he doing?" she asked. "Daddy, he makes me nervous. Please take me out of here now."

"I believe he's checking the license on their computer and getting other information about us," Joe piped in.

Mary pointed out, "I wonder if he thinks we are strange. Paul, please ask him why we were stopped."

"Yes, yes," Amy acknowledged. "I believe it's a specific computer that police use to text. Deaf people could use it to make calls like a telephone. I read an article about it in one of those magazines."

Mary asked Paul, "Didn't you mention purchasing one of those two months ago?"

"Yes, some deaf customers demanded we buy one for the bank," recalled Paul. "But our management found it unnecessary and ridiculous to spend that amount for something we'd rarely use. They rejected it."

Joe questioned, "But didn't you propose installing a ramp for people in wheelchairs at the bank's curb? And Sean, your friend, had Braille plates placed all over the walls for blind people. Did you find them useful?"

"Well," admitted Paul, "they were seldom used and cost us thousands of dollars. At that point, I felt they were somewhat unfair." Turning back to Mary, he pointed out, "But yes, darling, I told you about it. I agreed completely with them, because I didn't see any reason for us to get it. We would have wasted our money on that unnecessary device."

After a few minutes, the patrolman stopped typing and began to write on his clipboard. He quickly got out again and walked toward Paul's side of the car. Once he got there, he handed the clipboard to Paul. It said, "The interpreter is on her way to help us communicate with each other. She'll arrive in just a few minutes. In the meantime, I will fill out a ticket for you. My radar clocked you at fifteen miles per hour over the fifty-five-mile-per-hour speed limit. Please continue to wait for a few more minutes. Thank you."

The patrolman tipped his hat kindly, and then he returned to his car. The moment he got in, the flashing lights were turned off. He looked at the van to memorize the state and numbers from the license plate. After removing his hat, he began to write on the clipboard again.

Paul said with concern, "Looks like I was speeding without realizing it. He said he would fill out a ticket for me and that the interpreter is on their way to help with communication."

"That was the pager with texting I told you about," said Amy.

"Oh no," objected Mary. "I don't think we need an interpreter. We aren't illiterate! This is wasting our time; we could just write back and forth. I will fill out a grievance to the state about his unreasonable decision. Paul, why didn't you tell him that we are hearing and don't need the interpreter? Tell him we can read and understand his writing."

"I'm sorry, Mary," responded Paul. "I didn't have a chance to do that. Everything went so fast. And I—"

Paul was interrupted by Joe's impatient call for attention. "Look at that white car pulling over behind us and the patrol car! Is that the interpreter he told us would come?"

The officer promptly got out of his car and walked to the white car. A short and chubby lady quickly leaped out of her car before the patrolman could open the door for her. She didn't have any make-up or jewelry on. Her appearance was terribly sloppy, unprofessional, and unacceptable.

Amy spoke to herself, "I wish other men were as polite and respectable to women as he is."

The family was overwhelmed when the officer and interpreter began gesturing with their hands. Their faces showed that they already knew each other. After taking turns gesturing to each other, they glanced at the van in amusement. The family misunderstood their facial expressions.

Frightened, Toni said, "Daddy, it looks like they are fighting with each other. Please, I'm so scared." She began to whine.

Mary said, "Please don't worry, Toni. Everything will be OK." Turning to Paul, she asked, "Should you hop out and protest? It's not fair that we don't understand what they are talking about. Please ask them to include us in their conversation."

Amy put her arm around Toni, reassuring her. "They aren't fighting, Toni. They have to use their hands to communicate in sign language."

Paul pointed out, "Mary, honey, how can I communicate with them if I go out there? They might misunderstand and suspect I'm aggressive toward them. We must be careful and wait patiently."

Mary asked, "Why do they keep glancing at us with sarcastic smiles? It looks like they think we're stupid or something. I don't like it at all. It's not fair. The way they are doing that makes me paranoid, because they won't allow us to be part of the conversation. I feel so humiliated. Paul, please do something. See what they are talking about. After all, it's our right to know what is going on."

Again Paul protested and pointed out, "How in the world can I communicate with them, dear? You know I don't know how to use the language of sign. It's better for us to be patient and wait, like he told us. Please?"

Joe peeked at the officer and interpreter and hollered with excitement. "Hey, that lady is coming to us."

As the interpreter came closer, Toni began to lose control. She buried her head into Amy's lap.

"Hello," the interpreter said with a strange accent that sounded almost French. "I'm s-s-sorry, but I do not s-s-speak well. I am s-s-still training with my s-s-s-speech. However, I can hear well and will be able to unders-s-stand you if you s-s-speak s-s-slowly with large mouth movements. Please be pas-s-tient with me if I s-s-stop you and as-s-sk you to repeat for clarificash-shu-tion. My name is-s-s Wanda S-S-Smith." She even signed while speaking for the patrolman, which caused some awkwardness for both sides.

Paul thought that her s's sounded harsh and were very hard to understand. Mary spotted the label on her coat, which said, "Wanda Smith, Professional Interpreter." Next to the name, it said "level V." Obviously it showed the level of interpretation skill. Mary sighed and rolled her eyes.

Paul nervously began to talk fast, like he normally did. He kept turning his face and pointing at the patrolman and at the road. "I'm sorry, but he—the patrolman—didn't tell me why we had to wait for you to come. I think it's not necessary and a waste of time. I'll accept the ticket." As he tried to continue, he was startled when Wanda yelled at him to stop.

"Mis-s-s-ster, I am s-s-sorry, but you need to speak slowly s-s-s-so that I can unders-s-stand you. Pleas-s-se repeat from the beginning."

Paul was dumbfounded. He began to stutter his previous statement, nearly imitating the interpreter.

Wanda smiled nervously and asked him to relax. "I am s-s-sorry, but pleas-s-se repeat ons-s-ce more." As Paul attempted to restate his speech, Wanda suddenly interrupted. "That was fine. The patrolman is going to fill out the ticket for overs-s-speeding by fifteen miles per hour in the fifty-five-mile-per-hour s-z-s-zone." She turned to the patrolman and began to sign without speaking. Obviously she was covering for her incompetence.

Mary protested, "Hey, what are you talking about? Why aren't you using your voi—"

Paul covered his mouth with his hand, gesturing to Mary to shush. "Please, darling, let me do the talking. Please don't cause more problems now. I have decided to just nod and take the ticket. I promise you, as soon as we get back home, I will inquire all about that ticket, and I'll appeal if I must."

As the entire family except Toni watched and made wild

guesses of what they were talking about, Wanda pointed at Paul. She signed, *Paul said he understood and would accept the ticket.*

The patrolman signed, *OK, please wait a few minutes. I will go jot down a ticket.*

Speaking aloud, Wanda said, "OK, mis-s-ster, pleas-s-se wait while he—the patrolman—gets the ticket and your documents-s-s."

As expected, Paul accepted quietly. He said, "OK, we will wait."

Wanda and the patrolman walked back to the car. They signed at each other for a while, occasionally glancing at the family. This caused the family to feel somewhat uncomfortable. As the patrolman quickly shifted his head toward them, he smirked at their funny, curious faces. Amy sensed his amusement and felt embarrassed.

Joe piped in. "It looks like Toni is right. We should turn back and avoid that town. Daddy?"

"Joe," said Paul, "yeah, I agree with Toni. After the patrolman leaves, I will look at the GPS and see if there's a route going the other way."

"I don't like this," said Mary. "Along with being stopped for speeding, they have certainly humiliated us. I hope we won't find more people like them in that town."

Toni yelled, startling Mary. "Mom, like Dad and Joe said, we are not going to go to that town. Are we? I'm afraid of those people. One can't speak, and other one vocalizes unintelligibly. Please don't consider going to that town."

The interpreter suddenly approached the van, and the family readjusted in their seats.

"Mister?" Wanda muttered in a high, strange voice. "T-t-the patrolman will issue you a citation for s-s-s-s-s-speeding s-s-soon. Thank you for your patiens-s-ce. Do you have any question for him before I leave for another as-s-sign-n-n-ment in the town?"

Mary snapped back, "Yes, I do. All of this was unnecessary. I will report your incompetent skills in interpreting. And I know you both conspired against us, which was not fair. You—with your incompetence—obviously do not deserve another assignment."

Paul sank down in his seat.

"Oh, thank you for the compliments about our attitude and my being competent," Wanda responded innocently. She had obviously misunderstood Mary. "We try our best as professionals. We were talking about what a des-s-cent family you are awhile back. Good day."

Too quickly, Mary mocked back, "Th-th-thank you-u-u. Oh, you are wel-l-l-co-o-ome."

Paul sat up and said nervously, "Please forgive her—no—I mean us. OK, we will wait for the patrolman. Thank you for your help. Bye."

Wanda hopped into her car and rolled away after signing goodbye to the patrolman. The patrolman glanced at the family a few times while he continued to type on his device.

The family wondered what he was doing. When he stepped out of his car, they faced forward again, sitting up properly as if they were waiting courteously. The patrolman walked toward them with papers in his hand. He handed Paul his license and registration back with a nice message on the cover slip. It read, "Drive carefully, and have a pleasant ride in our state. Thank you." His flashing smile really attracted the family, especially Amy. He gestured for them to go on, waving with his Canadian hat.

Paul shuffled the papers, looking for the citation. In his amazement, Paul exclaimed, "My gosh! Instead of the citation with a fine, he only gave me a warning."

Amy grabbed the cover slip, assuming that the patrolman would say more. After turning the slip to the back, she screamed, and everyone jumped. Amy read the beautifully handwritten message. "Since it is obviously your first time in our state, I decided to issue you a warning this time. Good luck." Without their knowledge, Amy slipped the note into her small purse as a souvenir, her heart pounding.

Shortly after resuming their trip, they read a sign that said, "Deafiesburg, three miles." Strangely no one, including Toni, suggested to turn away from the city. They were simply stunned and quiet.

3

THE CITY OF DEAFIESBURG

As the family approached the city, Mary apologized. "Children, I was really wrong when I complained and mocked the interpreter, but I was disgusted. Please forgive me. But I will report that the interpreter was inept to the proper community service or whoever handles these situations."

Joe commented, "Mom, we understand your feelings, and we forgive you. Honestly we can't really blame you. We were wondering what that level five on her name plate meant. Was it her level of interpretation skills?"

"Agreed," Paul exclaimed. "She—whatever her name was—her job performance as an interpreter was terrible. I could not figure out how she got that level."

Everyone laughed, and they forgot to look at the GPS for an alternate route to avoid Deafiesburg. It seemed like they subconsciously wanted to go into the city.

"Yeah, Dad and I think alike again," Joe expressed excitedly.

Amy made a face and groaned. "Yeah, right, Joe."

"We're in the city now," warned Mary.

The sign read, "Deafiesburg city limit." Beneath that, in smaller print, was "Population: 275,000."

Toni nervously reached for Amy's hand. The family continued to be in awe of the beautiful scenery as they entered the city. The main street was a very wide, divided highway with three-way lanes on both sides. There were beautiful broken medians along the road, at every block. Strange, short green trees and colorful flowers surrounded in the medians. Paul glanced at the name of the highway, Benjamin Hirsch Parkway.

Two little girls, Toni's age, walked on a nice, wide cemented sidewalk, heading in the same direction as the family's van. They were animatedly signing while looking happy and peaceful. As the van passed them, the girls stopped. They had noticed that all heads inside the van were staring at them with open mouths.

Suddenly the girls leaped and waved, giggling at three boys rushing across the median on bicycles. One of the boys signed something, which caused one girl to laugh at the other's embarrassment.

The family exchanged looks and wondered what they were talking about. Toni whispered to herself, "Would it be rational to learn sign language to get to know them as friends?"

Suddenly Amy screamed, "Look at that sign!"

Startled, Paul almost lost control of the car. The sign said, "Deafyland State School for the Hearing and the Blind—three blocks." An arrow on the sign pointed to the left.

Mary murmured, "Why in the world would they have a hearing school with the blind?"

"What's the purpose of that school?" wondered Joe.

Passing that sign, Amy hollered, "Hey, here's another unpleasant sign."

The sign read, "Deafyland State Hospital." Beneath a dotted line was "Deafyland State Prison—five blocks" with an arrow pointing to their right.

Mary protested that it was offensive. "Why are those three institutions located close to each other?"

Suddenly a hot rod appeared from a small side street on the right-hand side and turned in front of the van. Frightened, Paul slammed on the brakes, causing the family to tumble around inside the van. The car was purple with artistic yellow and red flames on the sides. The engine roared loudly.

The driver was a young, good-looking boy who was obviously deaf. At first, he covered his mouth with his hand like he was trying to say *oops*. He raised himself higher over the window for Paul to see him say sorry. Then he roamed off.

Paul didn't understand what the boy was saying but considered him a reckless driver. Amy, on the other hand, thought the boy was cute and like some of her friends at home. The family continued to admire the scenery, but they thought the residents they had seen were like aliens.

Along the parkway, many houses were Victorian style

with beautiful matching colors, just like other towns or cities that the family had seen before. The lawns, bushes, trees, and flowers were very lovely and well cultivated. A sturdy, big-bellied gentleman stood on his lawn, holding a rake and listening to his bigger, fatter neighbor. The neighbor violently signed while sitting on his riding mower, his face stern. Their houses resembled each other, except for the colors. Paul wondered if the two men were arguing. In reality, the man on the riding mower was complaining about the rapid growth of weeds, as he did each week. He and his wife were tired of weeding them out so often. As the van slipped away, the family glimpsed the man with the rake animatedly moving his hands too, causing the rake to fall to the ground.

Paul exclaimed, "Look up ahead. We are approaching a roundabout in the highway."

The family observed a huge sign with a circular diagram that showed the names of streets cars could exit onto. One led back to the parkway. As they approached the circle, they were astonished to see a huge, eight-foot statue standing on a five-foot, beautifully carved marble base. The name on the statue—Benjamin J. Hirsch—was visible, but the inscriptions beneath and above the name were invisible. It appeared to be a memorial. Paul felt butterflies in his stomach as he recalled Mary reciting the town's history. The statue was very impressive. The sturdy gentleman was graceful with his right leg bent forward a little and his left stood straight. His left hand was resting in his coat pocket. His right hand was extended up high, next to the right side of his head. The family sensed that it was a gesture, like he was welcoming visitors. He had a smile on his face. It was common for men in his time to have a mustache or beard, but his face was clean-shaven. He had a woolen beret cap on. His clothes reflected the style that the men wore at that time he was alive. His physique looked strong and muscular through the clothes.

Amy whispered to herself, "That gentleman's face looked so wise and kind yet stern and very determined. He looked like he was content with what he saw and how the civilization he had left behind had evolved."

Toni vaguely heard her and asked what she was talking about.

Amy shook her head. "Oh, nothing."

4

THE ACCIDENT

PAUL WAS SO HYPNOTIZED BY THE STATUE THAT HE DID NOT pay attention to his driving and failed to yield the right of way. The front of an expensive-looking classic car crashed into the side of the van, where Toni was sitting. Toni's head slammed against the side window, shattering the glass. She fell over and passed out on the seat. Slivers of glass covered her. Amy was scared and panic-stricken. She tried to wipe the glass off Toni with her hands. Some glass splinters cut and stuck into Amy's hands, which started bleeding.

The rest of the family was all right. Paul and Mary were both upset when they realized that they were going to have more problems now with the professional deaf people. Mary felt so depressed but was scared when Amy screamed.

"Toni, wake up! Oh, no, my Toni. Please wake up!" Amy said, trying to shake her sister. Her hands smeared blood all over Toni.

Joe turned to the back seat and took Amy's hands off Toni. Paul and Mary quickly got out of the car. Paul tried to open the sliding door, but it was badly dented and stuck. Mary was right behind him, crying. They turned to seek help, but to their surprise, a patrol car and rescue van had already arrived.

The vehicles had decals on them that read "City of Deafiesburg Police Department" and "Deafiesburg Rescue Squad." The men and women that exited the vehicles had similar wording on patches on the shirt sleeves of their professional-looking uniforms. The crew was friendly and ready to help. The gentleman from the car that wrecked the van was also ready to help. He wore a neat suit.

Paul and Mary were so relieved to see help had arrived. They were ready to talk but were dumbfounded when the police officer began to violently sign with the owner of the car and the rescue crew. The owner of the car explained the accident to the policeman, who was ready to open his report clipboard. Paul was worried by the wild signing and urgent facial expressions. He suspected that the rescue workers were arguing. He didn't know what to do.

The rescue workers were actually communicating fluently and working together to develop a plan. Finally, the rescue crew gestured to the family to move out of the way. One crew member appeared with a huge, powerful tool that could push the sliding door out. As Paul and Mary backed away, the crew took Joe out of the van. A lady in a uniform was there, holding large pads and rolls of gauze in her rubber gloves. As soon as Joe was free, she climbed in the van and carefully wrapped Amy's hands. The lady then beckoned for Amy to step out, so the rest of the crew could to tend to Toni.

Suddenly the family heard a voice speaking in English right behind them. "You guys, don't worry. We are here to help you in any way. The owner of that car sensed that you were hearing and paged me to come the moment the accident occurred." The voice belonged to a professionally dressed interpreter. She was tall, neat, and intelligent-looking. "I am an interpreter. My name is Violet, and I will help with communication."

Amy instantly peeked at Violet's name tag, which had level three beneath. The family gave each other knowing looks. It made sense that Wanda was level five and Violet was level three. The family assumed that someone who was level one must be fluent.

Inside the van, Toni remained unconscious while the three rescue squad members quickly and efficiently assessed her. Other crew members and the family stood by, observing their work. The crew signed everything while checking on Toni. One of them was checking Toni's pulse; another was checking her eyes. The last one held a small black box with a digital computer in his left hand. A black wire led from the computer to a tool that looked like the end of a stethoscope. The attendant put that tool on Toni's chest to check her heartbeat. While he was doing that, instead of using sign language, he skillfully mouthed to the crew with his facial expressions and gestures. Except for the family, everyone including the interpreter understood what he was saying.

Violet spoke again, startling Paul. "Good news, the EMT

just said that Toni is going to be fine, but he suspects she has a concussion."

Amy wondered if the EMT was hearing.

Violet suddenly changed the tone of her voice to signify that a different attendant was signing. "I think we'd better bring her to the hospital for full observation. The doctors can confirm whether she has a concussion or not."

The rest of the crew nodded in agreement. Suddenly a stretcher was brought out, and the rescue team moved the crowd out of the way.

Mary began to weep. "Oh, my Toni." The rest of the family held her hands.

As the EMT attendant smiled and began to sign to the family in a professional manner, Violet translated. "Would any of you like to hop in the ambulance with her?" He pointed at Amy. "I also think that you should go too, so we can take care of your hands."

Mary quickly said that she would join both girls. After seeing that the EMT attendant was deaf, Paul silently questioned his qualifications and wondered if they should verify his credentials.

The female attendant who had taken care of Amy's hands smiled as she signed, and Violet interpreted. "I assure you, the girl is fine. She's starting wake up. By the way, is her name Toni?"

The family nodded.

Paul suggested, "You all go now. I'll check with one of the police officers about the accident report and the damage to the car. Then they can take me to the hospital to meet you. OK?"

"I will stay with you, Daddy," insisted Joe. It was automatically interpreted to the deaf crew. While the family members were talking to each other, they didn't realize that everything they were saying was interpreted to the deaf professionals.

The rescue truck and ambulance left with Mary, the girls, and the interpreter. Paul was startled when a policeman began signing to him, but a man in casual clothes appeared from nowhere and began interpreting for the officer.

"All right, let's take care of the report now," the man interpreted. "The sooner, the better. Then I will drive you to the hospital."

Paul felt so relieved that an interpreter had conveniently arrived. The interpreter quickly introduced himself as Bob. Paul and Joe were impressed that the communication between two different languages was going smoothly. They sighed with relief, realizing that Violet and Bob were both competent interpreters.

Paul thought to himself, *As I watch someone sign and listen to the voice interpret it, I feel like I understand the incredible language.*

The policeman signed, and Bob interpreted, just like Violet had. "I am David. Let's do the accident report now. The wrecker is on the way."

When the accident report was complete, the cars were towed away. Paul signed the report form, stating that he was responsible for the accident.

Bob interpreted as the owner of the wrecked car introduced himself. "My name is Jack." Jack gave Paul a card for the insurance business he owned and chuckled. He looked at Bob and signed while Bob interpreted. "If you like the idea, you are welcome to come to my office later, so we can do the accident paperwork. I assure you, it would not be a problem. It would be nicer and easier to handle the paperwork in an office." Bob explained that Jack's phone was a video phone and that they could communicate through a relay service.

Paul smiled and felt relieved. He realized that the friendly atmosphere, fair communication, and helpful professionals made him feel at ease, unlike some of the people in his hometown who can hear. But at the same time, Paul still felt confused and concerned about the history shared by Mary. He decided that if there was an opportunity, he would inquire about it.

Paul responded that as soon as they settled down in a hotel and learned the results of the wrecked car, he would call. Then he thanked Jack. Jack hopped into another classic car, which was driven by an attractive woman. Paul assumed she was Jack's wife. She flashed a smile at the crowd and rolled off. As they left, they were signing back and forth, obviously about the accident.

As Paul and Joe approached the police vehicle, David insisted that Joe sit in the front with him. He pointed to the back seat for Paul and Bob. He signed, and Bob translated. "Is it all right with you, Mr. Braden, if your boy sits in the front? I could explain some of the devices that we have on the dash."

Paul saw Joe's face light up in excitement. "Sure," he answered without hesitation.

David signed in ASL, explaining some of the devices, like the pager, VP machine, and emergency beeper, which worked fast and were very reliable. He trusted that Bob would peek over from the back seat to translate. Whenever Joe talked or asked questions, David would glance in the rearview mirror at Bob's translations.

The police communication system was all based on visibility and experience. David emphasized that research demonstrated that visually oriented equipment provided as quick of a response as auditory systems used in hearing police cars. Paul and Joe were impressed. They started to question their assumptions about the underachievement of deaf people but decided they needed more evidence to know for sure.

The city continued to be pleasant to Paul's eyes as the police car slowly rolled around various corners and down roads. Paul and Joe enjoyed observing David's fluent ASL and listening to Bob's professional and voice interpretation. For the first time, Paul glanced at Bob's nameplate. He noticed that Bob was level two. Paul quickly realized that he had the opportunity to ask if the first level was for the highest qualified and fifth level for the lowest. When he did, Joe turned to listen to Bob's response.

Bob chuckled. "No, it's the opposite of what you said, Paul."

Paul protested, comparing Bob's second level and Violet's third level with Wanda's fifth level. They all startled when they heard David's giggling voice. Paul continued, "Wanda, if I can recall her name right?"

Joe nodded in agreement

"Wanda was a terrible interpreter when the highway patrolman stopped me," Paul repeated. "We couldn't figure out what level five was, so we assumed it was the lowest qualification."

Bob was going to explain, but he promptly and respectfully backed off when David started to sign. Instead, he translated David's words. "Yes, you are right. Our leaders just started an investigation on those situations. They have selected an all-deaf committee to develop a better interpreter evaluation. I believe it will be done soon. The current evaluation was developed by a mostly hearing committee. At that time, politicians thought the hearing were the right ones to develop it. Now every interpreter will be required to take the new evaluation, and their level will be changed to an appropriate and fair one."

Paul and Joe were amazed.

Bob promptly signed and talked at the same time. "David, I would like to add something if that is OK with you."

David raised one of his hands like he had a gun, and gestured in a manner that said *shoot*.

Bob continued, "In addition to what David said, all agencies have already independently graded and prioritized the skills of every individual interpreter based on recommendations by hearing customers. They send interpreters out for serious or simple situations based on those grades."

David nodded in agreement.

Joe raised a good point. "Why did they send a bad interpreter on the highway when they knew she was terrible?"

Again David signed and Bob translated. "Sometimes we don't have any choice but to send the 'bad ones.' The best ones are usually busy with other important jobs, such as at hospitals, job interviews, doctor offices, lawyer offices, courts, and the police station. Someone who fails to pursue or pass the latest strict interpreter evaluation—especially the hands-on examination—would be terminated after the third attempt."

The father and son looked at each other and quickly realized that Wanda would eventually be reevaluated.

5

THE DEAFIESBURG COMMUNITY HOSPITAL

As THE POLICE CAR ARRIVED AT THE HOSPITAL, PAUL dropped his jaws in amazement at how gorgeous the front looked. It accentuated the giant figure-eight-shaped road and large parking spaces on both sides. Mini shuttle buses went back and forth, picking up and dropping off the visitors at the hospital's front doors. The wide, spacious white building looked sharp and sturdy, from the foundation to the fifth floor at the top. Paul also spotted a helicopter pad on the right side. It was ready to accommodate any emergency.

Paul and Joe glanced at each other like there were still many impressive sights to see. Their gut feeling was that the deaf people had done this unique and skillful construction all over the city. They were startled when they heard an interpreter's voice say that Toni was still in the emergency section. They promptly asked themselves where, what, and how the police knew about it. As the car followed the curve toward the rear of the building, where the ER entrance was, they experienced the most pleasurable sight of bright green grass and artistically arranged flowers. The car drove up to the front door of the ER.

Suddenly, a voice spoke, "Here we are."

On the sidewalks out front, some doctors and nurses walked, all communicating in sign language. For the first time, Paul knew in his heart how trustworthy the deaf professionals were. As his anxiety faded, he at ease at last felt. Now he was excited to see the girls.

As Paul and Joe entered the ER unit, they were immediately impressed with how things looked. The rooms, floors, walls, and offices were strictly clean, shiny, and well-sanitized. The friendly hospital staff walked around, serving patients. Paul and Joe felt like the patients were being well-cared for, not just at the hospital but at home as well.

Amy rushed toward them, looking happy. The first words Amy expressed were that Toni was fine and happy. After Paul noticed the tape and gauze around her hands, he asked how she was. Amy said she felt no pain and felt very clean. She led them to the room where Mary and Toni were. As they walked, the deaf staff went about their duties and completed assignments like busy bees. Everyone nodded and smiled like everything was fine. That made Paul feel relaxed and reassured him that Toni was all right, just like Amy had described.

When they got to the room, Amy opened the drapes.

Toni hollered excitedly, "*Daddy*, I'm fine. The people here have helped me a lot."

Paul saw all the bandages wrapped around Toni's head and felt a little distressed. Mary, sitting next to Toni's bed, remembered that the entire staff was deaf and that several excellent interpreters had shadowed every crew member to make sure the communication between them was in harmony. Paul sighed with relief after Mary reported that the doctor said Toni had a mild concussion but was going to be fine. He had suggested that she remain in the hospital overnight for observation, to make sure she was okay. If she did well, she would be released in the morning.

They sat around Toni's bed and chatted about their wrong assumptions of deaf people and the negative remarks they had made. Joe brought up how they would think of other interpreters who did the job well, including Wanda. They all laughed. Paul mentioned what he had learned from David and Bob about the deaf evaluators.

Joe questioned, "Do you think Wanda will get the necessary training to improve through mentorship."

They all agreed completely.

Amy wondered, "How many deaf people have suffered because the unprofessional interpreters gave them misinformation?"

Paul looked around and said, "Don't you agree that the deaf people are OK after all?" Everyone nodded. "I guess, since the van is in the shop, we could stay for a few days. Would you like that?"

"Yes, absolutely," said Toni.

Amy declared, "I think I will try to learn sign language, so I can make new friends without using my voice."

"Me too," declared Toni.

Paul was startled as he turned toward the open curtain and saw a deaf family. The father, mother, two sons, and daughter bore a strong resemblance to the Braden family, except for the gender difference among the children. The father had hearing aids in both ears, which were hidden behind his curly brown hair. His green eyes twinkled as he flashed the family a huge smile. The petite woman next to the father had beautiful strawberry-blond hair down to her shoulders. Her light blue eyes admiringly stared at her husband, and she smiled when he started to talk.

The Braden family was dumbfounded. Everyone's mouths hung open in astonishment. Suddenly Bob popped in from nowhere with a big smile on his face. He stood between the families.

As usual, the first sound was made by Mary. She began to say, "Who—" but stopped as Bob began to speak and sign simultaneously. He was interpreting for Peter Murphy, the father of the deaf family.

"Hello to the Braden family. I am Peter Murphy, and this is my sweet wife, Emily, and our three children. The oldest is Peter Jr. My little girl is Earlene, and last is my baby boy, Sam."

Everyone turned to Sam, who rolled his eyes. He was obviously annoyed with being called a baby. Then everyone turned to Toni, who giggled loudly. She was obviously at ease in the deaf environment.

Bob skillfully interpreted as Peter continued to sign. "We were sorry to learn of the accident you were in. We happened to come by for an appointment, and someone mentioned that you were going to stay at a hotel. My Emily asked me to offer for you all to stay with us while Toni is cared for by this hospital. We own a bed-and-breakfast. We could get acquainted with each other. I always tell everyone that our place is like a second home."

Everyone, even Mary, looked at Paul with pleading eyes, begging him to accept the offer. Paul glanced at his family. Everyone was startled again when Bob directed their attention to Peter Jr., who had the same shade of hair as his mother but green eyes like his father. He was as fit as an athlete. Amy's heart pounded rapidly as she looked at him. She thought, *What a dream boy he is.*

Bob translated Peter Jr.'s guess. "Mr. Braden, my instinct tells me that you are a golfer, correct?"

Paul felt flattered. He admitted that he loved to play golf but was not a pro. Joe interrupted and said that he played golf too.

Peter, Jr. concluded, "Hooray! We could play golf later if you all want to." He turned to his father. "We are going to have fun playing together if the Braden family is interested."

Peter Sr. nodded.

Bob translated, "Absolutely!"

As they were about to depart the hospital room, Mary turned to Paul and told him that she would stay with Toni.

Toni exclaimed, "Don't be silly, Mom. Go and have fun. I need to rest now." She smirked, feeling cozy. Then she turned to Amy and added, "Don't forget to visit tonight." She smiled at the deaf nurse who was checking on her vitals.

Mary shook her head and said, "Toni, I'm staying with you. You can rest, but I need to stay with my little girl."

Toni rolled her eyes and grinned at her mother.

Bob assured Mary that an evening interpreter would come in soon to help with her communication needs. Paul was so amazed by all the hospitality in this unique town.

6

THE MURPHY RESIDENCE

Paul, Joe, and Amy were in the Murphys' van as it approached the bed-and-breakfast house. The scenery continued to be pleasant. They were mesmerized by the beautiful landscape.

Bob, who sat on the rear bench, translated for Peter Jr. "On the right is the golf course. It's called Par Three Courses."

The course was impressively landscaped. Its flat and hilly surfaces were well arranged, and the green grass was well trimmed. The ninth hole was in the white sand, a bold, yellow flag planted in it.

With a sarcastic expression, Amy glanced at Peter Jr., trying to get his attention. "Is there a golf course for women somewhere?"

Everyone chuckled at the question, eager to receive his response.

Peter Jr. signed, *I'm sorry, Amy. Not that I know of. But at*

Par Three Courses, we welcome women to play, too, if they are interested. Would you care to play? He gave her a slick smirk.

After Bob had interpreted the message, Amy was happy that she had gotten Peter Jr.'s attention.

The Bradens were stunned when they saw the Murphys' house. It looked sturdy and beautiful. The curvy driveway led the vehicle toward a two-car garage and a big parking lot for guests of the bed-and-breakfast. Bob explained that everything had been designed by Peter Murphy. There were beautiful, colorful flowers along the driveway and well-trimmed bushes next to the garage. The beautiful two-story brick house stood to the left of the garage. The Braden family also noticed that the house had a lot of windows. They knew immediately that visitors in the past had always felt welcomed, like the Bradens were feeling at that moment.

Paul thought to himself, *The visitors probably had a hard time leaving and were tempted to stay permanently.*

Bob translated for the Bradens as Peter started signing. He explained that there was a beautiful park within walking distance that had picnic spots, a swimming and fishing lake, and a big playground. A lot of people used the park for a variety of events, such as picnics, ball games, and Frisbee. Peter suggested that Emily prepare a picnic basket, and they could go to the park to enjoy the goodies there.

The Braden family nodded and said they would enjoy that. Paul felt a sense of disappointment because Mary and Toni missing out.

Emily signed, *Let us show you to your rooms before we*

eat dinner. Unless you would like to get settled and rest before doing anything?

After Bob had translated, Joe shook his head and said, "We can bring in our luggage, but we don't need to rest. We've been sitting in the van all day."

When they entered, Paul was once again flabbergasted by the beautiful house. They could tell that it had been carefully thought out, with its elegant designs and handiwork. It looked like the designs and decorations were done by a professional. Peter Murphy had built the house, and Emily Murphy had picked out the colors, furniture, etc. The whole house looked like it was done by HGTV people or like it was from the cover of *Better Homes*. The Bradens fell in love with the house and were amazed that deaf people were capable of doing everything by themselves, as if they were normal.

Amy immediately felt at home when she was shown her room. It had a bay window, where she could sit and look out over the beautiful property. *I am going to read a book here tonight,* Amy thought. Her bed looked big and comfortable with its beautiful, yellow comforter with flowers. The sheets matched the comforter and the drapes. The room was sure to make any guest feel welcomed, happy, relaxed, and comfortable.

Amy heard a beeping sound and saw a small, flashing light on the TV screen across from her bed. Puzzled, she went to it. She saw a small slip of paper with instructions that read, "Press the red button to see a message." She looked at the bottom of the TV and saw a red button, so she pressed it.

Emily Murphy's sweet face appeared. She signed something that Amy didn't understand. Thankfully the TV was captioned. Amy was able to replay the message and read the captions. Emily Murphy had signed, *Dinner is almost ready. Come on down when you are done.*

The Braden and Murphy families settled around a huge, sturdy oak table in a beautifully decorated dining room. They enjoyed a delicious dinner that had been well-prepared by Emily. Peter and Emily had insisted that Bob eat dinner before his shift was over. Bob finally gave in. He enjoyed the meal before his replacement showed up.

Bob's replacement was a good-looking man dressed in a black top and denim pants. He flashed a friendly smile. Then he spoke and signed simultaneously. "Hello, everyone. My name is Tom. I will be your interpreter for this evening. Bob needs to go home."

Both families went into the living room and gathered around the comfortable couches and armchairs, which were arranged so every person could face each other directly. This was always expected when sign language was used.

Tom settled between both families, so everyone could see him clearly. He immediately explained, "Eye contact is very important in deaf culture. Deaf people need to have full access to communication."

Paul noticed the special arrangement of the furniture. He liked how they could also view the lovely backyard, which was lined with a white picket fence and beautiful flowers. He sensed that the Murphy family knew the Braden family had a lot of questions.

Tom translated as Peter smiled and began to sign. "Since you all are new to the town, do you have any questions? Please feel free and ask us anything. We aren't easily offended."

Paul chuckled and said, "I admit we were confused when we first got into town. We looked up information on the internet and found it very interesting. Some of the information was somewhat upsetting to us as hearing people. We felt offended by a few things mentioned in the history. But we are very impressed with what we have encountered so far. You've made us feel so welcomed. Why have we never really heard about this state?"

Peter smiled and signed.

Tom translated, "Yes, people who have no knowledge of deaf culture, world, language, or history would naturally get offended. We understand that. We went through the same thing when we were in your world. We faced barriers in our daily lives. We were offended and oppressed by hearing people. Don't get me wrong—we appreciate our interpreters, but some don't do their jobs as well as others. That has always been our main concern, so we try not to let it happen here. Bob and Tom are among those who are trustworthy and well respected. In the hearing world, we didn't always get interpreters and often got stuck with miscommunication or misunderstandings. Some businesses, doctor's offices, or events just wouldn't get an interpreter. They would tell us to bring our own. We decided that we wouldn't let hearing people experience the same issue here, because we wanted to be first-class in providing equal access."

Paul and Joe peeked at Tom as he spoke. They noticed that he had a small grin at the corner of his mouth. Paul wondered if the interpreter felt like he was being put on spot. He was fascinated with how Peter gracefully moved his hands and how Tom skillfully voiced what Peter was signing.

Amy kept thinking about how she would love to understand what they were signing. She wondered if she could learn sign language, so she could talk to Peter Jr. directly.

Peter Jr. waved to get everyone's attention. He signed, *Would anyone like to learn a few words in sign language?*

After Tom had translated, Joe and Amy immediately said, "Yes, we would love that!"

Paul chuckled and said, "Yes, we'd enjoy that. Do you mind if I ask where your children go to school?"

Tom began translating as Peter nodded and signed. "Yes, let me share the interesting history of deaf education."

Peter explained how proud he was of Deafiesburg's public education system. He explained that it was operated by a team of deaf members, including him. In the past, most deaf schools had been operated by hearing professionals who didn't know what was best for deaf education or didn't feel deaf children could learn as well as hearing children. The hearing professionals liked to experiment on the deaf children with different methods, like they were guinea pigs. Some of them even thought the oral method was the only option that would help deaf students learn. Hearing professionals disagreed with each other on which method was best, but most agreed that sign language was a bad choice.

Without Paul realizing it, his face indicated that he was slightly offended.

Peter immediately noticed and signed, *I can tell you are not one of them.*

After Tom had translated, Paul shook his head and said, "Definitely not. I can see that deaf people can function as normally as hearing people."

Peter smiled and signed, *Yes, thank you! My children attend the deaf school, and they love it there.*

Paul's phone rang. He took it out of his pocket and answered the call. He looked at Joe and Amy, saying, "It's Mom." Then he spoke into the phone. "How's Toni doing?" He spent a few minutes talking on the phone while Amy and Joe continued conversing with the Murphys. As he hung up, he looked up and said, "Toni is doing well. The doctors and nurses are not concerned, but she and Mary will still stay overnight. Mary said they had access to communication with the deaf professionals working at the hospital. They had great interpreters who made sure they got what they needed. Toni is also starting to feel comfortable with deaf people."

Amy noticed Peter Jr.'s puzzled look and spoke up. "Toni was scared when we got into town. She thought deaf people were strange."

Peter Jr. laughed and signed, *Yes, that's a typical response hearing visitors have when they come here.*

Paul pondered for a minute before turning to Peter. "I've often heard of a culture shock that people experience when they are in a completely different world and using a completely different language. I don't think we are experiencing that."

Peter nodded and began to sign.

Tom translated, "It's probably because you all came here with an open mind and heart. When people are willing to learn new things, they don't experience culture shock. They may feel awkward at times or confused, but with an open heart, they will get along just fine."

Amy smiled and said, "Well, Toni is an exception. She probably experienced culture shock."

Everyone smiled.

Joe shook his head and said, "Nah, she'll be fine. She'll end up telling us she loves it here."

Paul turned to Peter and said, "I believe we will need to call for a taxi to pick the ladies up from the hospital when Toni is discharged in the morning. Is there a taxi service in town?"

Peter shook his head and signed, *Nonsense. I will take you to the hospital.*

Paul thanked Peter before turning to Joe and Amy. "Let's start learning sign language."

After about an hour of lessons, the Braden family was able to practice signing by leading a conversation with the Murphy family using simple sentences. They practiced signing a few phrases: *Hello, how are you? What would you like to eat?* As expected, Joe asked to learn the signs for sports.

The Murphy family was very impressed with how fast Paul picked up sign language. He was doing even better than Amy and Joe. This made Amy and Joe determined to do better.

"Hey, Dad, I'm nervous. That's the only reason you're doing better," Amy said. She rolled her eyes as Paul's eyes twinkled at her mistaken word in sign language.

Paul shook his head and smirked. "Your old man has got a very good memory. I'm also a quick learner."

Amy rolled her eyes again and signed, *Oh yeah!*

The family continued practicing sign language for another half hour—mostly finger spelling the alphabet and numbers. Then they realized it was getting late and needed to get ready for bed.

7

A LONG DAY OF LEARNING ABOUT DEAF CULTURE

As the Braden family came down the stairs, they were greeted by the delicious aroma of breakfast cooked by Emily. Everyone was seated around the table, but they all stood up and greeted the Bradens. Paul, Amy, and Joe signed, *Good morning.*

Joe immediately poured a cup of hot coffee for his dad. Grinning, he said, "My dad cannot function without a cup of coffee in the morning."

Paul immediately noticed an unfamiliar face at the table—a young woman with beautiful black hair. She smiled as she stood up and introduced herself, signing and speaking simultaneously. "My name is Sarah. I will be your interpreter this morning."

Paul smiled and said, "Well, I hope I won't be needing an interpreter to communicate soon."

Sarah translated as Peter smiled and signed. "Yes, that

would be wonderful. It does take a while for someone to understand ASL. Anyone can learn basic signs, but to lead long and meaningful conversations, you will learn that ASL is a completely different language. With your abilities, I'm confident that you can learn fast if you fully concentrate on it. Some people have what it takes, and some just don't. I can see that you do!"

Paul nodded in agreement. "I would love to practice. I've always wanted to learn a different language."

They enjoyed another delicious meal prepared by Emily. They stayed around the table, chatting and joking. Before they realized it, nearly 2 hours had passed.

Paul turned to Peter. "I need to pick up Mary and Toni. I would love to bring them here and introduce them to your lovely bed-and-breakfast. What are your plans for the day? I also need to see about our van being repaired."

Peter nodded and signed, *We don't have many guests this week, so I'm fairly free today. I can take you to the hospital and then bring Mary and Toni here. If you want, I could take you to your van while your family stays here and relaxes.*

Amy stood up. She went to help Emily clear off the table and clean up the kitchen.

Emily shook her head and signed, *No, no. You're a guest. Go out and enjoy the beautiful day.*

Amy was thrilled, because she had understood most of what Emily had signed.

"Do you think Amy and Joe will be alright without an interpreter?" Sarah asked Paul, translating Peter's question as he drove down the long driveway and toward the hospital and pick up Mary and Toni.

Paul nodded and said, "Oh yes. It will be good for them to try and communicate with your wife and kids. Amy really wants to learn sign language."

He continued to enjoy the scenic ride as Peter drove him to the hospital. He was silent in his thoughts at the beginning of the ride. Then he turned to Sarah. "Peter, does your community welcome hearing people like us? Or is Deafiesburg only for deaf people? I was wondering because the majority here are deaf."

Peter smiled and signed.

Sarah translated, "That is a very common question. Yes, hearing people are welcome to live here. Many families have hearing children who live here. It's unusual for a hearing family without deaf members to live here, but they are welcome if they want to. We love hearing people. We know that the majority of them have good intentions and only want to help. It's just that we can do normal things and will only ask for help when needed."

Paul nodded. "Why is that unusual?"

Sarah translated Peter's answer. "This is a deaf world, deaf culture, deaf community. ASL is the primary language. Most hearing people would rather be in their world. It's just like us living in the hearing world—we would not be completely competent there."

Paul nodded and asked, "What about the school for

hearing children? Is there something special about it? We saw it as we passed through."

Peter smiled and signed, *Yes, there is a special school for hearing children. The school operates basically the same as our deaf schools but with an emphasis on English as the primary language.*

As they pulled into the circle in front of the hospital, Paul was surprised to see Mary and Toni outside, chatting with two nurses. His mouth dropped at the sight of Toni finger spelling and signing a few words. The nurses threw their heads back and laughed.

Toni must have said something funny, Paul thought.

Mary stood beside Toni, smiling from ear to ear. As Paul got out of the car, they ran to him and hugged him.

"This is the most amazing hospital ever! I love deaf people," Toni exclaimed breathlessly.

"What happened? What did you do to my daughter?" Paul joked.

Mary smiled and said, "We really enjoyed meeting all the deaf people here, and we learned some sign language. The doctor said Toni is doing great and is good to go. They took such good care of her. I'm no longer worried."

Paul shook his head. "I am so glad we got lost and ended up here. Let's go and see about our van."

As they started toward Peter's van, a handsome man stopped them. Flashing them a smile, he signed, *Remember me?*

It took Mary and Toni a moment to realize it was the highway patrolman that had stopped them for speeding.

Paul immediately recognized the man, even though he was dressed casually. He nodded and shook the patrolman's hand. The patrolman smiled and walked off.

As they drove away, Paul filled Mary and Toni in on everything they had done and how impressed he was with the bed-and-breakfast owned by the Murphy family. Sarah signed everything that Paul, Mary, and Toni said. Peter smiled as he drove them back to the bed-and-breakfast. Paul wanted Mary and Toni to get settled in and meet everyone while he checked on the van.

Peter drove Paul to the shop. While driving, Paul had a few more questions and thought it a good time to ask.

"Does the hospital always have interpreters?"

Peter began signing while Paul intently waited.

Sarah translated, "There is one staff interpreter at the hospital. She works forty hours a week. If a hearing patient happens to come after hours or there are multiple hearing patients, the hospital staff would call the agency to send more interpreters. Deaf people were forced to use video remote interpreting when we lived in other states. Some hospitals or doctor's offices would call for live interpreters, but others would force video remote interpreting on us. We disliked it because the laptop wouldn't always have a good connection. The video would often freeze. Sometimes we would have a hard time seeing the interpreter sign on the video. We decided we would only use video remote interpreting as a last resort in our state. We wanted to make sure that the hearing people who visit have full access to communication, especially in the medicine field."

"That makes sense. Technology is nice, but in person is always the best," Paul stated.

Exactly! Especially in hospitals or courts, Peter signed with emphasis.

<hr />

The Spotless Body Shop was where they had taken Paul's van after the accident. Paul was very impressed with the building and staff working there. Everything was in neat order, and the staff acted very professional. There weren't any hearing people working there. The lady at the front desk was very friendly and immediately took Paul to the repairman.

The van only had minor damages and could easily be fixed. The repairman said they needed one part, but it would take up to forty-eight hours to arrive.

When Paul broke the news to his family at the bed-and-breakfast, Amy, Joe, and Toni cheered loudly. Paul gave them a questioning look and asked, "Why are you so thrilled? Don't you want to go home?"

Joe shook his head. "No, we are having so much fun here. We want to stay longer."

Peter and Emily smiled when they saw the kids' reactions to staying longer. Peter waved to get their attention and signed, *Does anyone like to swim?*

Everyone nodded and raised their hands.

We have an Olympic-sized pool about two miles down the road, Peter continued. *It has a ten-foot-high diving board and a twenty-foot-high slide. Do you all want to go?*

Emily jumped in and signed, *We also have a softball tournament tomorrow. Practically everyone in town will be there. We thought you might enjoy seeing all the deaf people. There might not be many interpreters available.*

The Bradens turned to each other and smiled. Then Paul said, "Yes, definitely. We look forward to it."

Mary asked Paul, "Maybe you should call the bank and let your boss know we are going to stay here longer?"

Paul nodded.

Sam Murphy waved to get everyone's attention. *Do you realize you can talk underwater? Use sign language!*

Everyone laughed, but the Bradens took it seriously. They said, "Wow! I never thought of that!"

At the pool, the Bradens made a lot of new friends. They were amazed by how fun deaf people could be and how fluent the volunteer interpreter was at facilitating their conversations.

Peter Jr. boasted his skills by getting on the diving board when they first arrived. He gracefully dove into the pool, causing very little splash. Amy was quite impressed.

They swam and swam and talked and talked. The whole family attempted to sign some words underwater. There were a lot of laughter and learning experiences. Amy corrected Toni when she signed *swim* wrong, and Toni had to come up to the surface to laugh out loud.

Joe used a lot of gestures but only signed a few words.

Amy and Toni giggled at how Joe gestured. They blew bubbles because the moving water made his facial expressions even funnier. The Bradens learned so much about deaf culture by integrating with deaf people. They were exhausted and starving when it was time to go.

Paul turned to Peter and asked, "Can you recommend a fantastic restaurant we'd enjoy? I would like to treat you and your family to dinner."

After Sarah interpreted Paul's question, Peter smiled and nodded. He signed, *I've got just the place—The Jolly Palace. It's owned by a good friend of mine.*

They made a quick stop at the bed-and-breakfast so everyone could change clothes and then headed to the restaurant. Everyone was starving. Sarah had to leave for her daughter's dance class.

The Jolly Palace was a fantastic place to dine indeed. The Bradens loved how it was decorated and how bright the lights were. The whole restaurant looked cheerful. The aroma was mouth-watering. The waitstaff were all very friendly and professional.

A waitress who came up to their table signed so fast that the Braden family had to turn to the Murphys for help. Peter Jr. gestured and finger spelled what the waitress had signed.

Oh, I'm sorry. I didn't realize they were hearing. I'll get a hard of hearing waitress, the waitress signed slowly. She smiled cheerfully.

The Bradens decided to order steaks by pointing at the menu. Joe proudly finger spelled what drink he wanted. The rest of the family followed suit by. Mary tried to finger spell

Pepsi, but she used the letter *q* instead of *p*. Everyone laughed at her. Mary blushed and apologized. The waitress smiled and said she understood what Mary meant.

Amy grinned and slowly finger spelled slowly at Mary, *You want a qeqsi?*

Toni chuckled. "What kind of a drink is that?"

Mary laughed and rolled her eyes at the girls.

The steaks were very tender and juicy. The Braden family exclaimed that they were the best steaks they had ever tasted. A basket of homemade rolls was brought to the table and refilled frequently. The owner of the restaurant stopped by greeted them. He was glad to see Peter and his family.

I hope you are enjoying your visit here in Deafiesburg, and I hope the hospitality you're receiving is top, the owner signed smoothly.

Grace, a hard of hearing waitress, interpreted.

Suddenly the lights went out, and nightclub-style flashing lights came on. The Bradens were so confused, but Peter smiled and explained that it was somebody's birthday. Waitstaff surrounded one table, dancing and signing, *Happy birthday!*

The Bradens were stuffed and exhausted from all the excitement of the day. As soon as they arrived at the bed-and-breakfast, they bid the Murphys goodnight and went to bed.

The Bradens gathered in Paul and Mary's room to talk for a little bit before going to bed.

Amy sighed happily. "Wow, we truly had the wrong idea about deaf people. The ones here are nothing like we thought—they're so unique, intelligent, and warm."

Joe and Toni nodded in agreement. Toni turned to her parents and said, "I really want to stay a little longer. I want to learn sign language. I have never felt like I could fit in a minority group like I do here."

Paul and Mary looked at each other and smiled. Mary said, "I agree. I'm so glad we went off our route and ended up here."

Everyone nodded.

"I can't believe we thought so poorly of the deaf people," Toni exclaimed. "We thought they were dumb. They're nowhere near what we thought."

Everyone nodded again.

"Now I am curious about the athletes," Joe pondered. "I can't wait to go to the tournament tomorrow. I wonder if deaf people are good at sports."

"I'm sure they are. As far as we've seen, they're as normal as we are in everything else," Amy pointed out.

Paul nodded in agreement and said, "I am curious too. Tomorrow's tournament will be a good experience for us."

Everyone bade each other goodnight and happily went to bed.

8

ANOTHER EXCITING DAY
IN THE DEAF WORLD

THE NEXT MORNING, PAUL WAS WOKEN BY THE BRIGHT SUN shining through their windows. He was amazed by how full he still felt from the enormous dinner the night before. Emily Murphy offered to make breakfast, but Paul told her he wasn't hungry. He asked for something light to eat. The rest of the family nodded in agreement, wanting the same. They drank coffee in the parlor and enjoyed the sunshine. Then Emily brought them bagels and English muffins with cream cheese and a couple different flavors of jam.

Paul turned to Peter and asked about the local banks. He asked because he was very good at his job at his hometown bank.

Peter nodded and signed, *All local banks are fully staffed and run by deaf individuals. Most of them are college graduates with finance or business degrees. The banks are doing very well. Several deaf bankers have been invited to conferences in New York City. They even held workshops on banking.*

Paul was mesmerized as Peter explained how the banks were run in the state.

Peter continued, *If you would like, I can take you to visit a couple banks and introduce you to several of my banker friends.*

Paul was excited about the opportunity and said, "Yes, Peter, I would enjoy that."

Amy turned to Emily and asked, "What time does the tournament start?"

Emily said, "The softball tournament starts at 11 a.m. Maybe you should relax until a little before lunch time. I will prepare a picnic basket. Then we can go to the park and eat before the tournament."

The Bradens agreed and went to the living room. Joe took the TV remote and flipped on the TV. Surprised and confused, he said, "There's no sound!"

Peter Jr. smiled. *Look at the remote and press AA—that means auditory availability.*"

Peter explained, *Deaf people in the hearing world have closed captioning, so they can read what hearing people hear. Auditory availability allows hearing people to hear what deaf people see.*

"Do all the movie theaters in town have auditory availability?" asked Joe.

Yes, signed Peter Jr., *auditory availability is available via earpieces, which provide sounds for hearing people, so they can have equal access to movies and enjoy them.*"

Toni and Amy practiced signing with the Murphys while Emily and Mary worked on the picnic baskets. Amy shot Toni a dirty look when Toni was able to catch the language quicker than she was. Toni laughed at Amy for repeatedly making mistakes.

The Bradens and Murphys loaded the picnic stuff into the van and excitedly got in. The park closest to the tournament was about a ten-minute drive from the Murphys' house. Paul had requested that they not have an interpreter in the van or during lunch, because he wanted his family to practice communicating with the Murphys. Peter agreed. He could see that they were picking ASL up quickly. Not having an interpreter would be a good way for them to improve their skills.

Paul was once again amazed at how beautiful the park was. The landscape, trees, flowers, and huge pond filled with a beautiful flock of geese looked to be a perfect place to relax. Peter pulled into a parking lot next to a pavilion with plenty of picnic tables. Both families realized how famished they were. They quickly set the food on the tables and proceeded to eat. Toni saved some of the bread to feed to the geese at the pond. The others saw and did the same. The geese stared at them and started flapping around. It was obvious that they were hungry too and expected food.

As soon as the families were done eating, they cleaned up and went to the pond. The Bradens walked around, enjoying the fresh air and feeling so relaxed. They saw deaf families with young children playing at the playground and watched how fast their hands flew as they talked to each other in ASL.

The families' cheerful laughter were joyful to the Bradens' ears.

Using gestures, Paul asked, "Peter, was the park built and tended to by deaf people?"

Yes, it was opened shortly after the town was established, Peter slowly signed.

Paul was impressed by how the park looked. He thought the parks in his hometown could benefit from deaf people's creativity.

Amy started to finger spell but then pulled her phone out to type a message to Peter Jr. It read, "I'm a little nervous about going to the tournament. I hope the deaf people will be all right with hearing people attending."

Peter Jr. slowly finger spelled back. He gestured so Amy could understand what he was saying. *Of course. They are always glad to see hearing people.*

Peter told Paul that they would enjoy the tournament and that there might be a few interpreters available if they needed one. Some volunteers went to events like tournaments to help.

The Bradens were once again amazed as they pulled up the driveway that led to the parking lot for a couple baseball fields. The parking lot was already full of vehicles, and the fields were packed with players and fans.

Amy turned to Toni and said, "Wow, there is more than one baseball field here." Then she looked at Peter Jr. and slowly signed, *Will there be several games happening at the same time?*

Peter Jr. grinned and slowly signed, *Yes, it is a tournament.*

When they pulled into a parking spot, a group of people approached their van and waved, signing fast. The Bradens stared at their flying hands and were amazed by how fast yet gracefully they signed. When the Murphys and Bradens got out of the van, a couple players in uniforms approached Peter and Peter Jr. They gave each other high fives and started chatting.

Paul thought to himself, *The Murphys must be very popular.*

Whack. Amy stumbled as she turned to face the person who had hit her.

Oh, I'm so sorry, a deaf person signed. When he realized Amy was hearing, he voiced, "I'm so sorry. The hazards of ASL."

Amy could barely understand what he had said. His voice had been clear but hard to understand. People who are used to the deaf voice would understand him clearly. Amy politely nodded and waved goodbye. The guy grinned and took off.

That's the dangerous side of ASL, Peter Jr. signed slowly, gesturing with a small grin. *Our arms fly when we tell a story. If someone comes by, they get hit by us. I'm sorry you had to experience that.*

Everyone laughed, and Paul said, "Well, as long as Amy is OK."

The Bradens and Murphys kept walking. Occasionally the Murphys got stopped by acquaintances who were glad to see them. They came upon a table with a big sign that said, "Sign up and play in the tournament!"

Peter looked at the sign and inquired about it. Their past tournaments had not had this opportunity. The young man behind the table, a child of deaf adults, explained that a few teams were short players due to some conflicts. Peter asked him to voice his explanation to the Bradens. He did.

Joe asked Paul if they could sign up. Paul looked at Peter, who nodded. The young man explained that they would have to sign liability waiver. Peter Jr. and Peter decided to sign up too. They proceeded to play, ending up on two different teams.

A few hours later, the teams that Paul and Peter played for had beaten the other teams. So for the championship, it was Peter's team against Paul's team. In the last inning, the teams were tied. There were two outs, and Paul was at the bat. Peter was the catcher. Paul hit a long drive into the outfield. He rounded the bases and then slid onto home plate. At the same time, Peter caught the ball and tagged him. It was so close that even the umpire couldn't tell whether Paul was safe or out. Everyone on Paul's team said he was safe. On Peter's team, they said he was out. Everyone was arguing.

Peter asked Paul, *Were you safe or out?*

Paul was the only one who knew that he had been tagged a fraction of a second before touching the plate. He looked at the umpire and said, "I'm out."

Everyone on Paul's team was furious. They still believed

he was safe. Peter's team celebrated by yelling, jumping, and hugging.

Back at the Murphys' bed-and-breakfast, the men showered and got cleaned up for dinner. Paul received a call from the Spotless Body Shop, saying their van would be ready the next afternoon. When Paul relayed the message to his family, everyone looked disappointed.

Paul chuckled and said, "You guys don't want to leave, do you?"

They shook their heads.

Mary sighed. "As much as we've enjoyed being in a different world, we have to return to reality."

Amy threw her head back and smiled. She said cheerfully, "Let this be our new reality."

Paul smiled and said, "Well, we probably won't leave until the morning after, since we're getting the van in the afternoon. We could stay one more night."

Amy, Joe, and Toni cheered loudly. Mary started to tell them to be quiet but stopped when Amy teased, "Mom, deaf people wouldn't be bothered by the loud yelling."

Mary grinned and smacked her head.

Toni giggled and piped in, "I wonder what we are going to do tomorrow."

Joe turned to Paul and said, "The Murphys said something about going to a Bible study. Are we going with them or staying here?"

Paul shrugged. "I'm good with going with them. It's been a while since we last went to church. I'm curious what a deaf church is like."

Everyone nodded in agreement.

9

LAST FULL DAY IN THE UNIQUE CITY

THE BRADENS CAME DOWNSTAIRS AND WERE SURPRISED TO see a table full of deaf people they hadn't met. Paul looked at Peter quizzically. Peter signaled for an interpreter to come, and she immediately walked toward them.

"I am Margaret. I came with this group, and I'll be happy to interpret for you both," an older lady with an aura of kindness said and signed at the same time.

Peter began signing.

Margaret translated, "She is a child of deaf adults. She came with the deaf group from a town about an hour away. They came for the women's bowling event in town. Some of them are staying in hotels, but this group wanted to stay here."

"Does your town always have events?" Paul asked, chuckling.

Peter smiled after watching Margaret sign what Paul had said. *Pretty much, yes. Mostly in the summer.*

Amy turned to Mary and said, "Mom, you used to love bowling. Why did you stop?"

Mary smiled. "You happened. Life happened."

"Mom," Joe started, "you should play." He turned to Peter and asked if Mary could play.

"I don't think anyone can join at the last minute, but we could still grab a game or two. Would you like that?" Margaret translated Peter's quickly signed response. Then they introduced the Bradens to the people around the table.

The Bradens settled at the table to eat their breakfast. After discussing, they decided that they would play a couple games at the bowling alley. They got to know everyone at the table.

One deaf person piped in, *We should let Margaret eat.*

Margaret smiled and said she was fine with facilitating and eating at the same time.

The deaf person laughed and shook her head. *Well, that's how children of deaf adults are. They're so used to it after growing up in deaf families.*

Margaret smiled and nodded.

Toni asked Margaret if children of deaf adults ever felt stuck in between worlds. Margaret explained that all children of deaf adults came from different families. Not all deaf families were the same.

"However, I could probably speak for most children of deaf adults by saying that growing up in both worlds is one of the greatest experiences we could ever have," Margaret continued. "We can go back and forth. We are sensitive to deaf needs. We want to make sure deaf people don't feel left out. We were born interpreters. We experience the best of both worlds. I've met some children of deaf adults who didn't have a great experience, and I've met some who had the best. If I had to choose, I'd pick ASL and the deaf world in a heartbeat."

Peter added that depending on how much they can hear and how well they speak, some hard of hearing people feel stuck in between both worlds, not accepted by either. He also explained that it has gotten better for children of deaf adults and hard of hearing people.

Joe was deep in thought. He said, "We continue to learn new things about the deaf world. I'm so glad we got lost here."

———————

At the bowling alley, Paul was not surprised to see how big and charming the place was. There were many deaf people there. They weren't sure if there was a lane open for them, but Peter found one at the end of the room. They had fun playing a few games. Mary was surprised she was still able to bowl pretty well.

Peter Jr. turned to Amy and nervously signed, *Would you like for us to keep in touch after you leave for home? If yes, could I ask your dad for permission to do that?*

Amy giggled and blushed. "Yes!"

Peter Jr. smiled and looked around. Then he turned to Amy. *Where is your dad?*

Amy looked around and shrugged.

Toni looked at them and said, "Look over there, in the corner." She pointed and then giggled.

Amy and Peter Jr. turned and scanned the crowd. After a few moments, they finally found Paul standing in a circle of people who were chatting. He was watching the deaf people.

"Oh, how embarrassing. Isn't that rude? Didn't he and Mom always teach us not to stare?" Amy exclaimed.

Toni giggled.

Oh, it's OK. We are used to it. Trust me. Peter Jr. chuckled.

Amy pulled out her phone and typed, "Did you want to ask him now or wait until later?"

Peter Jr. nodded and stood up. He strolled over to where Paul was. Amy and Toni watched as he approached Paul. They looked at each other and giggled excitedly.

Paul turned when he felt a tap on his shoulder. As he came face-to-face with Peter Jr., he smiled

Do you understand what the people are saying here? Peter Jr. asked. He gestured slowly and finger spelled some words.

Paul shook his head and pulled out his phone to type on. He wrote, "No, but I love trying to figure out what they are talking about. I caught one or two words I recognized from the ASL lesson yesterday. I love watching them express themselves with their faces. It's so fascinating. Do you think it bothers them?"

Peter Jr. looked at them and typed in the phone, "It doesn't appear they even noticed that you are here. They are deep in discussion. Yes, we use our faces to express the tones of our emotions or to emphasize, like you do with your voice. You know when a person is mad or excited by their tone."

Paul finger spelled, *Yes, that makes sense.*

Peter Jr. smiled nervously and glanced at Amy. Amy gave him a quizzical look. He shook his head and shrugged.

Paul was very impressed with how their van looked when he went to pick it up. It looked new, like it had never been in an accident. Paul paid the owner and thanked him. As he walked to the van, he turned around to examine the building. He studied how the deaf employees worked together effortlessly. He smiled and thought, *Do they ever go wrong?*

At the deaf church, the Braden family was awed by how the church looked. It was huge and had a gym next to it. When they entered, they were greeted by bright lights and loud music, which was mainly bass. Paul turned to Peter, who found a volunteer interpreter to explain that deaf people love to feel the vibration since they can't hear.

In the hearing world, the deaf often don't have access to churches due to lack of interpreters. Peter explained that because of this, the deaf in their community wanted to make sure that the hearing had full access to messages shared in church. Paul immediately felt a pang of guilt for his bad thoughts about the deaf and how they weren't important in the hearing world.

Both families entered the auditorium and saw that the room was packed with deaf people. A man came up to the podium and started to clap the music's rhythm, matching the bass drum. The Bradens could feel goosebumps on their arms. They were used to normal hymnal songs sung in churches but had never experienced something like this. Peter explained that they had traditional singing and group-led singing, but they also enjoyed the bass drum like at a basketball game. After some clapping, a preacher came up and thanked everyone for coming. He started preaching a simple message about gospel.

The Bradens listened to the interpreter and studied the preacher's signing. They thought there was no way they could ever become translators. Paul inquired about it later, and Peter confirmed that it is harder to translate sign language than any other language, because sign language is the only language that is purely visual. Other languages were both verbal and written, but ASL was neither. Interpreters would have to know exactly what a deaf person meant in specific phrases and regional signs or expressions.

The preacher only preached for fifteen minutes, but his message was spot on. Paul enjoyed it immensely. After the service, everyone went to the next room to eat and socialize. Paul felt bad, because they hadn't brought any snacks to share. Peter told him not to worry about it. Paul glanced at his family and smiled, thinking how intrigued they were with the deaf world. Then he suddenly noticed Peter Jr. and Amy slowly signing together and giggling.

Paul glanced at Mary, catching her watching him and

smiling. Paul pointed to Peter Jr. and Amy and shrugged. Mary laughed. She knew what he was thinking.

The Bradens had a great time eating and playing basketball in the gym. Amy was impressed by Peter Jr.'s athletic skills while he was with Joe. It was getting late when they decided to go back to the bed-and-breakfast.

10

GOODBYES ARE HARD

AFTER BREAKFAST ON THE BRADENS' LAST DAY IN THE MOST interesting city ever, both families sat in the parlor to chat for a little bit. The Bradens looked sad, because it was time to go home.

Paul got up and signed, *Bathroom.*

Amy nodded at Peter Jr. and raised one eyebrow, hinting that it was his cue.

Peter Jr. nodded and got up, following Paul into the hallway. While following Paul, he pulled out his phone, opened a blank note, and typed in it. He chose this method of communication because wanted to make sure the conversation was clear and without misunderstanding.

Paul turned around when he heard footsteps behind him. He was surprised to see Peter Jr. following him. He stopped and looked at Peter Jr. curiously. Peter Jr.'s hand was shaking as he typed on his phone. Paul noticed and wondered if he knew what Peter Jr. was going to ask.

Peter Jr. shoved his phone into Paul's hand nervously. Paul read the message: "I was wondering if I could have your permission to stay in touch with Amy when you guys leave town?"

Paul stared at Peter Jr. for a moment. Then he grinned and signed slowly, *Yes, that would be fine with me.*

Peter Jr. stared at Paul. Paul threw his hands out and laughed. After realizing that Paul had granted permission, Peter Jr. grinned. He signed, *Thank you!*

Paul and Mary went up to their room to start packing. Paul said, "You won't believe what Peter Jr. asked me."

Mary smiled. "I think I have an idea."

Paul confirmed Mary's suspicions. "Well, you figured it. He asked for permission to stay in touch with Amy."

"That's sweet. Do you think they will actually stay in touch?"

Paul shrugged. "Who knows? I guess we will see." He turned to look at Mary. "I must admit that it is impressive. Boys don't really ask for permission to date these days. The boy back home—what was his name—never asked."

Mary nodded. "Well, if they do stay in touch, I would be OK with that. Peter Jr. is a very kind and respectful young man. We all would need to be fluent in ASL though." After a few minutes packing, she turned to Paul and asked, "Where are the kids anyway? Have they packed?"

Paul raised his eyebrows and shrugged. "I know they went to the arcade game room, but I don't know if they've packed yet. We should probably get ready to leave."

Mary nodded. She turned around to go to the game room and find the kids.

In the game room, Peter Jr., Earlene, Sam, Amy, Joe, and Toni played several games together. They were chatting and laughing when Mary and Paul entered the room. Paul was touched at the sight and thought to himself, *They are going to miss the Murphys.*

"Well, well, kids, have you packed yet?" Mary asked in a loud, booming voice.

The three Braden kids were startled as they turned around to see their mother in the doorway.

"Mom, it only takes me a few minutes to pack," Toni protested. "I promise. I just want to play more."

"We were talking about how we thought deaf people were quiet and didn't make loud noises," Amy explained. "Peter Jr. and Sam made fun of us. They said deaf people are loud. They can't hear themselves and don't realize the sounds they make."

"I never thought of that. But from what I've seen and heard, I don't think they're that loud," Mary pondered out loud.

"OK, kids, let's get packed and say goodbye," Paul said from behind Mary.

After some protesting, the Braden kids reluctantly left the game room to pack.

························◆·◆·◆·◆·◆·◆························

An hour later, the Murphys and Bradens were outside by the van. Paul had just come from the office, where he had paid for their stay at the bed-and-breakfast—with a huge discount as insisted by Peter. They started saying their goodbyes, which seemed to take forever.

Bob, the interpreter, was already there for a meeting that Peter had scheduled for later that day. The Bradens had more questions for the Murphys. Paul wanted to know if there were museums in the state. Peter confirmed there were many good ones on deaf history and important deaf people.

Grinning, Peter turned to Bob and signed, *Deaf Standard Time is a well-known phrase when it comes to trying to leave or arrive on time. We just chat and chat, losing track of time. I think that's what you're experiencing now.*

Paul laughed and said, "Well, I have no problem with that."

After they said their goodbyes, the Bradens thanked the Murphys for their wonderful hospitality and for making them feel welcomed. They exchanged contact information to stay in touch.

On the road, Toni became teary-eyed and said, "I can't believe I'm so heartbroken about leaving a city."

Joe nodded. "We did have such an educational and amazing time here."

Amy nodded sadly.

Mary turned to the kids and said, "I'm so sorry for the negative things I said about deaf people when we first arrived. It was wrong of me. Sure, I didn't know much about them, but that did not give me the right to complain and talk bad. They didn't deserve it."

Paul nodded. "I am sorry too. I am so glad I turned the GPS off and accidentally ended up here. It gave me a lot to think about. It helped me see the world in a different light. I think God brought us here for a purpose. I wonder about the deaf people who have not moved here. Are they happy in our world? Do they get equal access to everything, like they do in Deafyland?"

Amy nodded and said, "That really breaks my heart. We took them for granted. Deaf people are considered handicapped, but they really are not. At least not to me."

Joe stared out the window at the beautiful scenery for a moment. Then he murmured, "It makes me think of other disabled people. People in wheelchairs or who are blind—they all have something in common: the English language. Like Peter said, ASL is a visual language, not spoken or written. Deaf people are unique. They are not disabled."

The entire Braden family agreed with Joe's comment. Paul glanced at his children through the rearview mirror. Then he glanced at his wife. He smiled and asked, "What was your favorite part about our visit here?"

Mary sighed and looked at Paul. "Oh, I can't pick just one. Everything was great."

"Mine was signing underwater," Toni said, giggling. "That was so cool. Hearing people could never talk underwater."

Joe chuckled and said, "Well, for me—well, I'll let y'all guess."

Paul peeked at Joe through the rearview mirror. "The tournament, eh?"

Joe nodded. "Dad, you know it! But, really, like Mom said, everything was great."

Everyone turned to look at Amy, who smirked.

"Peter Jr., Peter Jr.," Joe said in singsong voice. Everyone laughed.

Amy blushed. "Well, I can't help it. He's so handsome and sweet."

After gasping from laughing, Toni looked at Paul. "Well, Dad, what's yours?"

Paul sighed and looked straight ahead for a few seconds before speaking. "That is hard. It was such an educational time for me. The tournament was great. I enjoyed playing with the deaf. Really, I loved every moment." The family was silent for a moment before Paul continued. "So, kids, where do you want to go for vacation next year?"

"Deafiesburg, Deafyland," All three kids said in a loud, singsong voice.

"I thought so." Paul chuckled, glancing at Mary.

"I figured," Mary said. "I would love to come back. Maybe we could go to different cities around the whole state. We could visit each town and see what they have—go to their amusement park or something like that."

"I love that idea. Can we ask the Murphys to take a vacation and show us around?" Toni asked.

Amy pondered for a minute. "I wonder why the news never talks about this state. We barely hear about it. When we do, it's usually something like, 'There's not much to talk about.' I'm pretty sure all my friends back home don't know much about the state either. That isn't right. The whole country should know about this amazing state."

Joe nodded. "We should change that. We should tell the whole world about the amazing deaf state and the fun deaf people."

The whole Braden family voiced their agreement. Then they heard a beep from Amy's phone. Amy looked at it and smiled.

"Peter Jr.?" Mary inquired.

Amy nodded, blushing. "Oh, how can I wait a *whole* year before we come back? I don't think I can wait that long."

Paul laughed and said, "We could split my vacation throughout the year."

"Yes, yes!" Joe and Toni yelled at the same time.

Arthur Grant Dignan was born to deaf parents and spent his childhood in Jacksonville, Florida, where he attended the Florida School for the Deaf and Blind. After graduating there, he experienced odd jobs before entering Gallaudet University, where he met the love of his life, Joyce. There he earned a bachelor's degree in Sociology, then went on to add Master's degrees in Social Work and Deaf Education. These scholarly accomplishments and his notable persona created high demand for Arthur to fill educator or administrator positions all over the nation in Deaf schools. Later, he went on to teach American Sign Language at the university level. Additionally, Arthur wrote a weekly newspaper column, conducted workshops, and entertained audiences with his one-man comedy shows, many of which are captured on video. His most recent character was in Deaf Missions' production, "The Book of Job" (2018). All his professional successes aside, his greatest triumph, pride and joy is his family: Joyce his bride of 50 years, their three children and spouses, and twelve combined grandchildren plus countless extended family members and close family friends. Arthur's faith has carried him through his life, and he is always found standing for the old hymn, "Onward, Christian Soldiers".

Printed in the United States
by Baker & Taylor Publisher Services